A WOODLAND MYSTERY™

The Good-for-Nothing Dog

A WOODLAND MYSTERY

By Irene Schultz

The Wright Group®

To Benita Livingston, my kind, dog-loving friend

The Woodland Mysteries™

The Good-for-Nothing Dog
©1996 Story by Irene Schultz
Cover and cameo illustrations by Taylor Bruce
Interior illustrations by Meredith Yasui and Charles Solway
Map illustration by Alicia Kramer
©1996 Wright Group Publishing, Inc.

The Woodland Mysteries were created by the
Wright Group development team.

The Wright Group
19201 120th Avenue NE
Bothell, WA 98011

Printed in the United States of America

10 9 8 7 6 5 4 3 2 1

ISBN: 0-7802-7238-2

What family solves mysteries...has adventures all over the world...and loves oatmeal cookies?

It's the Woodlanders!

Sammy Westburg (10 years old)
His sister Kathy Westburg (13)
His brother Bill Westburg (14)
His best friend Dave Briggs (16)
His best grown-up friend Mrs. Tandy
And Mop, their little dog!

The children all lost their parents, but with Mrs. Tandy have made their own family.

Why are they called the Woodlanders? Because they live in a big house in the Bluff Lake woods. On Woodland Street!

Together they find fun, mystery, and adventure. What are they up to now?

Read on!

Meet the Woodlanders!

Sammy Westburg
Sammy is a ten-year-old wonder! He's big for his fifth-grade class, and big-mouthed, too. He has wild hair and makes awful spider faces. Even so, you can't help liking him.

Bill Westburg
Bill, fourteen, is friendly and strong, and only one inch taller than his brother Sammy. He loves Sammy, but pokes him to make him be quiet! He's in junior high.

Kathy Westburg
Kathy, thirteen, is small, shy, and smart. She wants to be a doctor someday! She loves to be with Dave, and her brothers kid her about it. She's in junior high, too.

Dave Briggs

Dave, sixteen, is tall and blond. He can't walk, so he uses a wheelchair and drives a special car. He likes coaching high-school sports, solving mysteries, and reading. And Kathy!

Mrs. Tandy

Sometimes the kids call her Mrs. T. She's Becky Tandy, their tall, thin, caring friend. She's always ready for a new adventure, and for making cookies!

Mop

Mop is the family's little tan dog. Sometimes they have to leave him behind with friends. But he'd much rather be running after Sammy.

Table of Contents

Chapter 1:
The Wild Thing

Someone was kicking the back door, hard.

Mrs. Tandy heard the noise.

She ran to open the door.

There stood fourteen-year-old Bill Westburg. In his arms he held a dog ... a dusty black dog.

Tail and all, it was about two feet long. Its legs were skinny, like a baby goat's.

It was as dirty as a pig in mud ...
with a mostly fuzzy body
and a hairy face
and a fox-like tail
... and a star of white fluff all around its black nose.

Bill said, "Quick, let me into the kitchen! I have to put this wild thing down, before he bites me."

Mop, their little tan dog, took one look at the new animal.

He began to shake. He gave a couple of yips.

He ran to Kathy's bedroom. Then he dived under the bed.

Mrs. Tandy said, "Well, Bill, what kind of critter do we have here?"

Bill set the dog down on the kitchen floor.

It ran under the table.

Just then, Bill's brother Sammy and his sister Kathy appeared.

They heard a noise ... like toenails scratching the floor.

Ten-year-old Sammy bent down for a look under the table. He said, "Hey! What's that? A monkey?"

The dog thought, "Who's that funny kid?"

Kathy, thirteen, said, "What did he do to Mop? The poor thing's hiding under my bed!"

Dave Briggs, sixteen, rolled into the kitchen in his wheelchair.

They all lived together as a family. They called themselves the Woodlanders.

The new dog stuck his nose out for a quick look.

He disappeared under the table again.

Dave said, "Whose is he?"

Bill said, "Nobody's. Well ... I guess mine now."

Mrs. Tandy said, "How did you end up with him?"

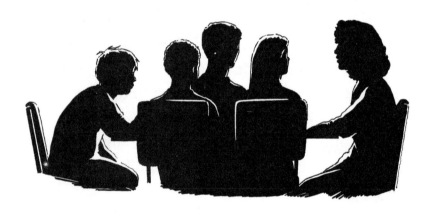

Bill said, "Well, you know Dave drove Mop and me to the vet's for Mop's shot. Just yesterday afternoon.

"While we were there, Dr. Silver told me about a dog whose owners didn't want it.

"That bothered me ... a lot. When you lose your parents like we did, you learn one thing for sure ... how important it is to have a family who wants you.

"Dr. Silver said the dog's owners wanted him put to sleep."

Sammy said, "Put to SLEEP! That means KILLED! Why did they want to kill him? Is he sick or something?"

Bill said, "No. He's not sick. They just didn't want him anymore, the vet said. And she told me where they live.

"So today after school I went to take a look at the dog.

"He was tied to a big post in their backyard.

"There were four little kids, all running

around him and screaming.

"One was about two years old. She kept falling on top of him.

"The mother told me the dog's mean. She said he snaps at the little girl. And growls at the other kids.

"She said he's just a good-for-nothing dog. She even called him Dumbhead. That's what they NAMED him!

"Then one of her boys hit the dog on the back. Of COURSE the dog growled.

"Then she said, 'This animal's out of control! I'm getting rid of him TODAY!'"

Sammy said, "I HATE her. Didn't you just HATE her?"

Bill said, "Well, I sure hated what she let her kids do to him. So the next thing I knew I was telling her I wanted the dog.

"Right then and there she un-hooked him. She said, 'Pick him up. He's yours, but I want my chain.'

"She said they were out of dog food. They've been feeding him bread for the last couple of days.

"So there I was, holding twenty pounds of dog.

"And I had books to carry. And I was seven blocks away from here!

"Partway home he wiggled loose. He made a dash for an open garbage can. He came up with half a sandwich ... ham, it looked like.

"Then he ate a paper napkin. I grabbed him when he finished that."

Mrs. Tandy bent down to look under the table. She said, "My lands, he's as skinny as a toothpick!"

Kathy put some canned dog food on a plate.

She put the plate near the table leg. They all heard sniffing.

Sammy said, "Good. He smells it. Maybe when he eats it we can get a good look at him.

Suddenly the dog dashed out from under the table.

He bit at the dog food. It stuck to the plate.

So he kept hold of the food ... and

8

pulled the whole plate under the table.

Sammy said, "ROTTEN RATS! I hardly saw him! Hey, what's wrong with his nose?"

Bill said, "Nothing. It's just his marking. He has a star of white hair all around his black nose."

Dave said, "He reminds me of the star-nosed mole in my science book. If we keep him we could call him Mole."

Kathy said, "I feel sorry for him. Let's call him something nicer than Mole. He's been hurt so much, he should at least get a good name."

Bill said, "Well ... how about Star Nose? That's pretty good."

Sammy said, "OK, I like Star Nose all right. Here, Star Nose!"

But the only thing that came from under the table was a growl.

Mrs. Tandy said, "Well, there's a star-nosed, dirty, growling dog in the house.

"And I was thinking ... if we keep him, what about poor old Mop?

"Will he spend the rest of his life under Kathy's bed?"

Chapter 2:
Poor Mop

It was time for dinner.

The Woodlanders all helped carry dishes and food into the dining room.

They had to walk back and forth into

the kitchen. Every time they did, a growl came from under the kitchen table.

As soon as they sat down at the dining-room table, they heard a lapping noise.

Dave said, "Listen! He must be out from under the table! He's drinking from Mop's bowl!"

Suddenly they heard a loud clattering sound.

Bill said, "Hey, what's he doing?"

They raced in.

There was Star Nose, standing on the kitchen counter.

He was wolfing down a stick of butter from a plate.

He looked at them with wild eyes and growled.

Bill said, "That's OK, boy. You must be starving. You can have it. We aren't going to hurt you."

Mrs. Tandy said, "What a jump he made to get up there! The kitchen chairs are all pushed up to the table.

"He must have leaped all the way up from the floor to the counter!"

Sammy said, "He should be in the dog Olympics! He'd win the standing broad jump!"

Kathy said, "Too bad there isn't a butter-eating event for dogs. Look, he ate it all!"

Dave said, "How do we get him down without him biting us?"

Kathy went over to the cupboard.

She took out a box of crackers.

She fed one to Star Nose.

With her other hand, she gently touched the dog's head.

Star Nose thought, "This tastes pretty good. Salty. But I wish she wouldn't touch me."

He gave a little growl.

Kathy held up another cracker for him to see.

She patted his head again.

This time he didn't growl. He just grabbed the cracker.

He snuffed up the crumbs again.

Then he sniffed at Kathy's fingers and licked the salt off of them.

Sammy said, "Look! He likes you! Let me give him one."

So Sammy fed a cracker to Star Nose, too.

Then Kathy put a cracker down on the floor.

She clapped her hands and called, "Here, Star Nose!"

Star Nose took a good look around at them. He finally decided no one was going to hurt him.

Like a cat, he jumped down from the counter.

He grabbed the cracker. He ran under the kitchen table with it. They heard him munching it down.

A few seconds passed.

Then slowly a black nose came into sight.

It stuck out a few inches from the shadows under the table.

Everyone was afraid to talk ... afraid they'd scare him.

A minute passed. Then a whole head came out.

Then out came a dog neck, and half a dog body.

Slowly Kathy lowered herself down to the floor.

Slowly Sammy, Bill, and Mrs. Tandy copied her.

Star Nose sneaked out some more, just a tiny bit.

Finally he was out all the way.

He sniffed at each one of them.

Then he sniffed at Dave's feet, and the footrests of his wheelchair.

Dave patted his lap and said softly, "Good boy. Come on up, it's OK."

And then ... Star Nose stood up on his hind legs!

He put both paws on Dave's knees. He let Dave pet him.

Dave said, "Look. I've never seen a dog do that! He's SMILING! It's weird!"

Star Nose's mouth was open. His lips were turned up at the sides.

Bill said, "It's weird, all right, but I

LOVE it!"

Kathy said, "He must feel a lot better now."

Mrs. Tandy said, "Well, I'D feel a lot better if some one WALKED him.

"So far in the last hour he's eaten half a ham sandwich ...

a paper napkin

a whole can of dog food

a quarter-pound of butter

... and four crackers."

Dave said, "Hmm ... I guess he does need to go out."

Bill said, "I'll take him. I think he'd come with me."

So Kathy patted Star Nose's head to keep him calm.

Bill snapped Mop's leash onto Star Nose's collar.

Star Nose followed Bill straight out the door.

Sammy said, "Poor Mop. We'd better get him out from under the bed.

"He hasn't had his dinner yet.

"And he probably thinks we like this new dog better than him."

He ran to get Mop.

He lured him out with a cracker.

Then he brought him into the kitchen and fed him.

After that, Mop lay down in his dog bed near the back door.

But Bill came in the front door.

He didn't know Mop was out of Kathy's bedroom.

He took the leash off of Star Nose.

Star Nose ran into the kitchen.

He took one sniff.

Then he dashed over to Mop, lying still on his bed.

He went straight for Mop's throat!

And he didn't let go!

Chapter 3:
A Dog Tornado

Mop YIPPED.

    Sammy yelled, "YIKES!"

    Mrs. Tandy shouted, "MY STARS!"

    Kathy cried out, "STOP HIM!"

Dave called, "THROW SOME WATER ONTO THEM!"

Bill ran to the sink.

But before he could do anything, Star Nose had let go.

He jumped away from Mop, and stood watching him.

He woofed.

Mop leaped out of his bed. He danced over toward Star Nose.

Star Nose jumped at him and took hold of Mop's throat again.

He let go again.

Then Mop did the same thing to Star Nose.

Star Nose thought, "Hey! I like this game!"

The dogs sniffed noses.

Suddenly Mop jumped at Star Nose and bumped against him.

Star Nose began to run. Fast!

Mop shot after him ...
out of the kitchen
through the dining room
down to Mrs. Tandy's room
back again
to the other end of the house
around Dave and Bill's bedroom
up onto the boys' beds
back to the living room
up onto the couch
... and back through the dining room.

The dogs barked. They yipped. They woofed. They skidded.

They slid. They jumped. They bumped. They raced.

Their toenails clicked on the wooden floors.

Sammy yelled, "It's a dog tornado!"

The animals rushed through the kitchen.

Star Nose smelled some bread. He

23

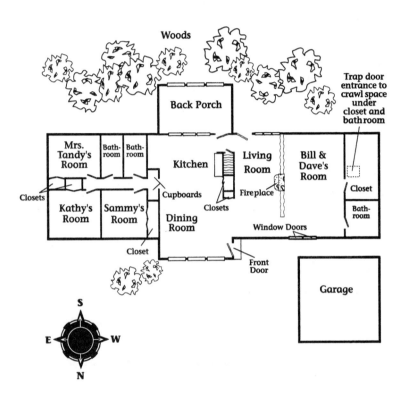

jumped onto the table.

He grabbed a bagel.

Mrs. Tandy started laughing. She said, "I've heard of a beagle hound, but this is a BAGEL hound!"

They had been so worried, pretty soon they were ALL laughing.

Sammy said, "I thought he was going to KILL Mop, right in front of our eyes! I was scared!"

Bill shook his head. He said, "Well, we have to stop them. They're bumping into everything in the house. They could get hurt."

So the Woodlanders spread out down the hallway and waited.

The next time Mop ran by, Sammy caught him and held him up in the air.

Poor Mop. He wanted to keep on running. His little legs kept racing, as if he were still on the floor.

He was panting and gasping.

His tongue hung out.

He was shaking all over.

Star Nose ran up to Sammy and Mop. He danced around on his hind legs. He barked right toward Sammy's face.

Then he ran back to the kitchen and dashed under the table.

Sammy said, "Boy, I guess he doesn't trust people yet. Really the only one he trusts is Mop ... but he's wearing Mop out."

Bill said, "Well, I guess we can't keep him. But at least I can find him a good home."

Kathy said, "I'll help you. We all will."

Mrs. Tandy said, "First things first. What do you think we should do with him tonight? We can't let him run Mop to death."

Dave said, "I'll take Mop out for a walk. As soon as we leave, get Star Nose down the basement steps. We can fix him a bed downstairs."

Mrs. Tandy said, "There's a big cardboard box down in the laundry room. Let's put an old blanket into it. He can sleep on that."

They fixed a bed for Star Nose under the clothesline.

Bill led him by the collar straight into it.

And Star Nose jumped right out of it!

So Sammy went upstairs for some doggy treats.

He put them onto the blanket. Bill led Star Nose back onto it. Star Nose ate the treats.

And then, he jumped right out again.

Star Nose thought, "I'll never stay in this dumb box!"

Kathy said, "Let's go up. Close the door to the basement and leave him. Maybe he will go to bed by himself."

Mrs. Tandy nodded.

Bill said, "OK. But let's take turns petting him first. Then maybe he will start trusting us.

"I'll fill a water bowl for him down here."

So they sat down on the floor and called to Star Nose.

He came over to them. He held his

legs stiff, ready to run. But he stood quietly and let them pet him.

Then they heard Dave come in upstairs with Mop.

Bill said, "I hate to leave Star Nose, but we should go on up."

They left Star Nose whining on the steps.

Mrs. Tandy closed the door.

She said, "I think he will be fine once he calms down.

"After all, how much trouble could he possibly get into down there?"

Chapter 4:
The First Morning

They didn't hear a single bark from Star
Nose all night.

Saturday morning Bill woke up early.

He saw Dave was still asleep.

He slipped out of the bedroom.

He was going to the kitchen, to listen for Star Nose downstairs.

He found Sammy already standing there at the door to the basement.

Then Dave wheeled into the kitchen. He said, "I was only half-asleep. I was going to check on Star Nose, too.

"I'll meet you in the basement!" He rolled out the back door, down the outside ramp.

Then Mrs. Tandy and Kathy walked in. Kathy was carrying Mop.

She laughed and said, "Looks like EVERYBODY'S checking on Star Nose! Just let me put Mop out on his chain."

Finally they went downstairs.

Star Nose was gone.

His box was empty.

Even the blanket was missing.

But the whole basement floor was covered with shirts.

Bill said, "Look! He's pulled all the shirts off the line and dragged them around!"

Mrs. Tandy said, "And that's not the worst of it. Look at this shirt. He's chewed off every last button."

Bill said, "What a weird dog! Do you think he swallowed them?"

Sammy said, "Look, his blanket's gone. Think he swallowed that, too?"

Bill said, "Of course not. It's around here somewhere."

But they couldn't find it in the laundry room. They went out to the main part of the basement.

Mrs. Tandy called loudly, "Here, Star Nose! Here, boy!"

They heard a noise coming from the basement bedroom.

They rushed in.

There on the bed lay Star Nose, looking droopy. He moaned a little.

His head rested on his paws.

He was lying on top of his blanket.

Dave said, "How in the world did he get that big blanket up onto the bed?"

Bill said, "Boy, is he smart! He made his own sleeping place!"

Sammy said, "Uh-oh. Listen to him! Now he has the hiccups. And he's burping. I guess those buttons didn't go down too well."

Kathy said, "Quick, get him out the

basement door! I think he's going to throw up!"

She was usually right about things like that.

So Bill grabbed Star Nose's collar. Sammy pushed him from behind. They moved him out the basement door and up the ramp to the yard.

Kathy ran out to bring Mop in.

A few minutes later Sammy led Star Nose back into the basement.

The hiccups had stopped.

Sammy said, "He must feel a LOT better … he started growling at me again. Whew, Kathy, we were just in time! Ick!"

Mrs. Tandy said, "Poor critter. He needs some good dog food. Look, you can see all his ribs."

Dave said, "Well, before we take him upstairs, how do we keep him and Mop from ripping apart the house?"

Sammy said, "Maybe it won't be so bad today. Maybe they got used to each other yesterday."

Mrs. Tandy said, "Let's see if they've calmed down at all."

So they all went upstairs.

The two dogs did sit down calmly ... for about two seconds.

Then they were off again!

They began to run next to each other, like race horses.

Dave said, "Quick! Let's get their food out!"

The dogs smelled the food. They skidded into the kitchen. They gobbled their breakfast.

They licked their own plates.

They licked each other's plates.

They licked the floor all around both plates.

They each took a big drink of water.

They went back to the plates and
started licking all over again.

At last they were done.

They lay down in the dining room.

Pretty soon Sammy said, "Listen to
them. They're both snoring."

Dave said, "While we have a chance,
why don't WE eat breakfast?"

Sammy said, "Saturday's a special day.
So let's have a special breakfast.

"How about pizza ... and cole slaw ...
and oranges?"

Mrs. Tandy said, "Why not! I'll turn
on the oven. Someone, slice oranges."

Kathy said, "I'll get a pizza from the freezer. And there's slaw from last night in the refrigerator."

After they had eaten, Mrs. Tandy said, "I want to open the front door to air out the house. I'll just leave the screen door closed."

Bill said, "OK, guys. We have to work on finding a home for Star Nose."

Sammy said, "Yeah, let's make a list! Write down that we should ask all the neighbors if they want a dog. And the kids at school."

Dave said, "We could run an ad in the Bluff Lake newspaper."

Mrs. Tandy said, "I'll ask at the garden club meeting."

Kathy said, "Let's make a big poster about Star Nose ... and put it up in the drugstore."

Dave said, "And we could make a

bunch of smaller posters, too ... to hang all over the place."

While they talked, the two dogs lay snoring in the dining room.

Then a cheery voice called from the front door, "Hi, folks! I've got a surprise here for you!"

Chapter 5:
Where Are They?

Kathy cried, "The mail's here!"

The mail carrier was standing at the front door holding a box.

Mrs. Tandy called, "Come right in,

Cinda! Do you have time for some cookies and a cup of coffee?"

Cinda walked through the dining room. She put a box down on the kitchen table.

She said, "Thanks! I can't really stop. But if you don't mind, I'll take a cookie with me."

As she got to the front door she called back, "I like your new dog! He grinned at me! Never saw a dog that could grin.

"Bite? Yes. Grin? No."

Bill said, "We like him, too. But he and Mop are too wild. They're quiet out there now because they're stuffed ... but you should see them the rest of the time!"

Cinda said, "But they're not out here, Bill. When I came in they shot out the door like a couple of bullets."

Bill said, "Oh my gosh."

Cinda said, "I'm awfully sorry. I didn't know you wanted them inside."

Sammy said, "Uh-oh. Poor Mop! He doesn't know how to find his way home. Every time he sneaks out by himself, he gets lost."

Cinda said, "Well, I'll be on the lookout for them. Sorry!"

And off she went.

Mrs. Tandy said, "Quick, let's give Chief Hemster a call and report the dogs missing. He can help find them!"

Dave said, "Hurry! Let's take the car and go look for them."

Kathy was worried.

She said, "What if we can't see them from the car? What if they're running through backyards?

"What if they get hit by a car?

"What if—"

Bill broke in. "They'll be OK, Kathy.

Sammy and I can check the backyards on foot.

"You and Mrs. Tandy ride in Dave's car with him. Get out at every corner. Call Mop's name. The dogs will hear you."

Dave said, "Let's meet back here every hour till we find them."

So as the car drove off, Bill and Sammy started walking.

Every time they saw someone, they asked, "Have you seen two small dogs? One's black, with white around his nose. The other is tan. A cairn terrier."

At last a woman told them she HAD seen a black dog.

She said, "But he smiled, like a little dragon! I got scared. I was afraid he was crazy, so I shouted GET AWAY!

"He ran off in that direction." She pointed.

At the same time, Dave, Mrs. Tandy, and Kathy were driving around town ... screaming their lungs out.

"HERE, MOP! HERE, STAR NOSE! HERE, DOGS!"

Every hour they went back to the house to report, "No luck."

By noon they had searched every block in town.

When they met back at the house, they were a MESS!

Mrs. Tandy, Kathy, and Dave were hoarse from shouting. They could only whisper.

Bill had lost the pocket off his shirt. It was back in someone's yard, hanging on a thorn branch.

Sammy was the worst mess of all.

His clothes were torn.

His shoes were filthy.

His hair was full of twigs. They stuck out all over like pins.

But nobody had the dogs.

Chief Hemster drove up the driveway.

He was the family's best friend. He took one look at their five sad faces and said, "Go wash up. I'm taking you to the Mexican place for lunch. We can talk about this there."

They felt a little better after stuffing themselves with tacos.

Chief Hemster said, "My officers and I will keep looking for Mop and Star Nose.

"And I've spread the word to the Office of Public Works. The city workers are watching for them, too.

"Who knows? The dogs may even come back on their own!

"Why don't you stay home until around four or so. That way we can phone you if we find them."

Bill said, "That's not a bad plan. We can get our homework out of the way while we wait."

By 4:00 the dogs were still missing.

So the Woodlanders searched outside until dark.

By 10:00 that night, worn-out and sad, they climbed into their beds.

Three hours later the phone sounded like a scream in the night.

Sammy flew out of bed to answer it.

A voice said, "We've got your dog and his friend, too. You can come and get them now if you want.

"Drive to the main gate at Lake Land Navy Training Station.

"But I'm warning you ... when you see these animals, you may not want them."

Chapter 6:
Dead Fish and Donuts

Sammy hung up the phone.

Everyone had rushed into the dining room.

Sammy said, "The dogs are found!

They're at the navy station!"

Bill yelled, "Yipee! What are we waiting for? Let's go!"

Five minutes later they were driving through the dark night.

Dave said, "Do you realize the navy station is over three miles away? It's a real mystery. How could such little dogs have walked that far?"

Sammy said, "Speaking of mysteries, listen to this. The man said when we see the dogs, we may not want them.

"What do you think he meant?"

Mrs. Tandy said, "They're probably full of burrs, and dirty. But I'll be glad to see them anyway."

They came to the gate.

Dave said to the sailor standing there, "Hello! We've come to get our dogs."

The sailor grinned.

He said, "We would have called you

sooner except for one thing ... no one on the base would go near them ... so we didn't know whose they were.

"So we just put them in a pen. We gave them donuts and some water.

"Finally a young guy who used to raise dogs helped out.

"He went close enough to read the little dog's tag."

Kathy said, "Were you afraid of them because the black dog grins?"

The sailor said, "No, that's not why we wouldn't go near them. Here, see for yourself."

He opened a gate to the yard.

Out ran the two little dogs.

Bill held out both hands to pet them.

Like a track champ, Star Nose LEAPED into the air.

He landed THUD in Bill's arms.

He smiled and breathed right in

51

Bill's face.

Bill almost passed out. He gasped, "Good GRIEF, Star Nose! You STINK!"

He dropped him to the ground.

Sammy had run up to pet Mop. "P-U! What a SMELL! Mop, you're disGUSTing!"

The sailor laughed.

He said, "I told you you might not want them. They must have walked up here from the beach.

"It looks like they ate rotting fish all the way. And rolled on them, too."

Bill said, "Dave, did you get a whiff of these pigs? How are we going to get them home? They'll stink up your station wagon!"

Mrs. Tandy said, "Don't call them pigs. A pig is a sweet-smelling rose next to these two."

Dave asked the sailor, "Do you have any old newspapers? We need something to protect the car."

The sailor said, "How about a big piece of plastic?"

Dave said, "That should work."

Kathy said, "I'll ride in the back seat, facing backward. That way I can lean over it, and hold them by their collars."

Sammy said, "Then I will, too. If you can do it, I can do it."

So they loaded the dogs onto the plastic sheet.

Sammy held tight to Mop's collar with his left hand ... and held his own nose with his right hand.

At home they phoned Chief Hemster and told him the dogs were back.

Then Mrs. Tandy said, "How should we wash these two?"

Dave said, "Let's do each one in a tub by him self. They might get wild if they're together."

Sammy said, "Boy, I'm going to scrub the tubs to death when we finish! I don't want to end up smelling like rotten fish!"

Bill said, "Well, Sammy, why don't you and I do Star Nose?"

Sammy said, "OK. But what do we do about his breath?"

Mrs. Tandy said, "That smell will go away in a few days."

Kathy said, "The smell isn't the worst problem. Here's what's worse. These dogs are full of dead fish and donuts.

"Tonight we might have TWO dogs

throwing up.

"I'll let Mop sleep in my room. If he starts making funny noises I'll run outside with him."

Bill said, "And I'll sleep in the basement bedroom. If I put Star Nose's blanket next to the bed, I'll be able to hear him.

"But right now, let's get the burrs out of their fur."

Mrs. Tandy got two little pairs of scissors from her sewing box.

They took the dogs into different bathrooms.

They ran the water.

Star Nose thought, "They want to give me a bath? They'll be sorry!"

Sammy said, "You hold Star Nose still, Bill. I'll cut out the burrs. That way I can hold my nose with one hand."

At last he said, "I think I've got them

all out. How should we lift him into the water? What if I pick up his front end and you lift his rear?"

Just then Star Nose took a running jump ... and belly-flopped into the tub.

The boys were soaked.

Bill said, "Look at this bathroom. It's worse than the shower in the school locker room.

"This dog is a MESS! Well, at least he can't do anything wrong while he's sleeping."

They finally got him washed, and put him downstairs.

It was 3:00 in the morning by the time everything was cleaned up.

The Woodlanders dragged off to bed.

Two hours later Bill dreamed a horrible dream ... that he couldn't breathe ... and was covered with rotten fish.

He woke up a little at a time. The horrible smell from his dream got worse instead of better.

He opened his eyes.

Star Nose was on the bed! He was lying nose-to-nose with Bill.

The dog was snoring and blowing his

fish breath into Bill's face.

Bill jumped out of bed. He shouted, "This is the last straw! I've GOT to find a home for this dog-gone dog!

"TODAY!"

Chapter 7:
Who Wants a Dog?

ᵀt was Sunday morning.

By 8:00 the Woodlanders were outside with Star Nose.

They were all dressed up.

They were talking to neighbors, asking if anyone wanted a dog.

They rang the bell only at certain houses ... ones where it looked like someone was already awake.

Bill said, "If we wake people up, they'll get mad. They might say no even if they need a dog."

Some houses had Sunday papers on the sidewalk. They figured those neighbors weren't up yet.

Star Nose was looking much better. He was shiny-clean from his bath.

Kathy had tied a blue bow to the top of his head.

Mrs. Tandy held him on Mop's bright red leash.

Sammy called, "Be sure to keep him about ten feet away from everyone. We don't want him to breathe on some poor guy ... and kill him!"

By noon they had covered four square blocks ... with no luck.

Mrs. Tandy said, "Let's go home and make lunch. How about making toasted sandwich pies?"

Sammy said, "Hooray! Perfect!"

So they went home and tied Star Nose out on the back porch.

Mop barked when he heard them coming. He yipped at their heels when they came into the kitchen.

Kathy and Bill took out the left-overs from the refrigerator. They put them on the kitchen table.

Just then they heard a knock on the front door.

It was Chief Hemster.

Sammy said, "Come right in, Chief. You'll get to see Mrs. Tandy all dressed up! And eat lunch, too!

"What's in that grocery bag?"

Chief Hemster said, "A treat to celebrate the dogs being found."

Sammy took one look inside.

Then he hurried with the bag into the kitchen.

He shouted, "Quick! Mrs. Tandy! Your BOY friend is here. And he's brought four quarts of chocolate milk!"

Mrs. Tandy grabbed the bag. She put it out of Sammy's reach, high up on the refrigerator.

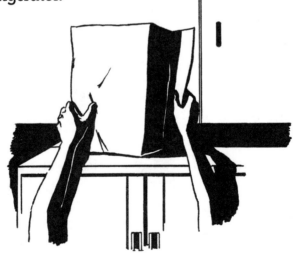

She said, "If he's my boyfriend and he's brought this, I guess it's for me. You probably wouldn't want any."

Sammy said, "Maybe I was wrong. Maybe I shouldn't tease you and call him your boyfriend all the time."

She handed the package back down.

Sammy grabbed it and ran into the dining room giggling.

He called, "He's not your boyfriend ... he's your SWEETIE-PIE!"

Chief Hemster pretended to chase Sammy around the dining-room table.

But in one minute Sammy was back in the kitchen, looking over the fillings for the sandwich pies.

Kathy laid out twenty-four slices of bread on six plates.

She said, "I think we can eat two sandwiches each."

Bill, Sammy, and Dave took charge of

the left-overs.

Mrs. Tandy, Kathy, and Chief Hemster were in charge of the round toasters.

They buttered the insides with a butter brush.

For his first invention, Sammy mixed left-over canned peas with tuna and mayonnaise.

He spread the mixture onto bread and put another slice on top.

He held the sandwich out for Mrs. Tandy to toast.

Then Bill came up with orange marmalade, cream cheese, and spaghetti.

Kathy toasted that sandwich.

Dave stirred up a mixture of sardines and mashed potatoes.

Chief Hemster sneaked a little taste.

He said, "This is actually pretty good!"

Now Sammy was getting into a real cooking mood. He came up with a mix-

ture of chopped hard-boiled eggs, sour cream, green onions, and more sardines.

Dave mixed sour cream, mashed potatoes, grape jelly, and string beans.

Bill said, "Check this one out! This is going to be the best!"

He put together tiny chunks of ham with chopped eggs and honey mixed into mashed potatoes.

Sammy said, "You stole my idea! Well, wait until you see THIS!"

In a bowl he mixed what was left of every single left-over!

As he tossed them in, he called, "Sardines! Ham cubes! Sliced olives! Chopped eggs! Spaghetti!

"Tuna! String beans! Mayo! Cheese chunks! Grape jelly! Mashed potatoes! Sour cream! Butter! Honey! Marmalade!

"And chicken gravy from a jar you guys missed!"

Then he stirred in a lump of peanut butter. It made a brownish, grayish, lumpy, sticky mush.

Then he actually TASTED it.

He licked his lips and smiled.

He took another taste.

He said, "Yum!"

So Kathy tried it.

She said, "It's GOOD, Sammy."

There was enough for six sandwiches of that.

They ate their sandwiches with chocolate milk. They gave little tastes of everything to Mop.

On a special plate they put tastes of everything for Star Nose.

Then they went out to give it to him.

But the chewed-off end of a red leather leash was all they found on the porch.

Star Nose was gone!

Chapter 8:
This Is an Emergency!

Sammy said, "Here we go again! Dog hunting!"

They hurried to the garage to get into the car.

But the moment they got to the front porch, Bill said, "LOOK!"

He pointed at the driveway.

There lay four big rolled-up Sunday newspapers, slightly chewed.

STAR NOSE!

There he was, trotting up the street. He had another paper in his big fishy mouth.

Bill said, "He's got a paper route! But instead of delivering them, he's un-delivering them."

He called, "Here, Star Nose! Here, pup!"

He ran down the driveway.

But Star Nose dropped the paper and danced away.

Just then a motorcycle came up the street.

Star Nose stood on stiff legs, waiting for it to come near.

Then he dashed after it, almost touching it.

He came back and tipped his head to one side.

He smiled a big smile.

Dave said, "Look, he's so proud of himself! He wants us to tell him how smart he is."

Sammy said, "SMART? He thinks he's SMART?

"He almost got himself KILLED!

"And he's got five neighbors thinking WE steal newspapers!

"And ... NOW WHAT'S HE DOING?"

A neighbor's cat was wandering up the street.

Star Nose stood as stiff as a statue. His tail stuck straight back. He held one paw in the air. He aimed his nose straight at the cat.

The cat saw him.

It ran up a tree at the edge of the driveway.

Star Nose jumped right after the cat, onto the first branch.

The cat took one look and ran to the very top of the tree.

The Woodlanders dashed down the driveway.

Dave stopped his wheelchair right below Star Nose.

They all looked up at the dog in the tree.

They called him to come down.

Star Nose looked up.

He thought, "That next branch looks too high to reach."

So he jumped down ... right into Dave's lap.

He licked Dave's face with his still-fishy tongue.

Then he curled into a ball and

snuggled up to Dave's stomach.

Kathy said, "Look. He thinks you're his own private pillow."

Dave said, "How could I stay mad at such a funny dog?"

He scratched Star Nose behind his fluffy ears.

Bill said, "Now we know all his tricks, so we know what to expect.

"I guess he isn't really bad, just a terrible pest.

"Kind of like Sammy here."

Sammy socked him.

Bill went on. "First we have to find out who owns all these news papers. Then we take Mop with us. He needs some exercise.

"But we leave Star Nose at home. That way he can't pull any tricks and kill his chances of finding a home."

Sammy added, "Yeah, by breathing on some one."

Kathy said, "But we have to tell the truth to any one we try to give him to ... that he IS a terrible pest.

"It wouldn't be fair just to dump him on some nice person."

Bill said, "OK, OK. But instead of saying PEST, let's say he's very active. Let's say he gets into a little trouble some times."

Mrs. Tandy said, "A LITTLE trouble!

74

Hah! I just hope he doesn't eat the furniture while we are gone!"

They went back to hunting for a new dog owner.

They walked around almost all afternoon with no luck.

Finally Dave said, "It's about five. Let's go to this one last house."

As they walked up to it, Sammy said, "I really think this guy Mr. Johnson might want him. He loves to hunt.

"And he already has that brown-and-white hunting dog.

"In fact, I bet he would LOVE another dog. A dog that can climb trees!"

So they knocked on the door and told Mr. Johnson about Star Nose.

Mr. Johnson said, "Sorry, kids. Sorry, Becky. Most dogs that make good hunting dogs are BRED to be hunters."

Sammy said, "Then this dog would be

75

perfect! Once he ate nothing but BREAD for days! He loves bread! And bagels!"

Mr. Johnson said, "No, what I mean is, good hunters usually have parents who are good hunters.

"They are usually pups from some sort of hunting dog. A pointer like mine. Or even a little terrier like the one you have there. Some special breed."

But Bill said, "Mr. Johnson, this is an EMERGENCY!

"We HAVE to find a person to take Star Nose.

"We can't keep him. And if we take him to the pound, they could kill him.

"I'll tell you what. If you'll just TRY to train him to be a hunting dog, I'll weed your big flower bed over there."

Sammy said, "And I'll mow your lawn tomorrow."

Mr. Johnson said, "Well ..."

They could see he still couldn't decide.

Mrs. Tandy came to the rescue. She smiled and said, "And I'll bake you a Dutch apple pie.

"You've had my pies at the Fourth of July dessert stand. You know what they taste like."

"SOLD!" said Mr. Johnson. "You'll find my mower in the shed, ready to go, Sammy. Bring the dog over tomorrow morning before school.

77

"I'll give him a try at hunting for pheasants."

They headed for home.

They felt really happy ... until they went inside.

Chapter 9:
Star Nose Goes Hunting

Star Nose was nowhere to be found.

They looked everywhere.

Then Bill called his name.

Star Nose bounced out of the front closet.

Mrs. Tandy said, "Why in the world was he in there?"

Dave said, "I bet he didn't know it was us coming in. He was hiding."

Sammy said, "Some guard dog!"

Then Sammy walked into the kitchen. He whispered, "Wow."

Star Nose had pulled open a cupboard door.

The garbage can was out from under the sink, lying on its side.

Garbage was spread all around the floor.

Next they saw that Star Nose had dragged the basement blanket up to the kitchen ... along with some clothes and a rug.

Mrs. Tandy stepped on the rug as she went to pick up the mess.

Her heel landed on something under it ... something soft that was lying on top of something hard.

She said, "ISH! What's under this RUG!"

Bill ran over to her.

He lifted the rug.

He said, "Holy cow! I guess Star Nose didn't want to eat without us.

"He covered his food bowl with this rug. That's what you stepped in!"

Bill said, "It doesn't seem like he knows what to do when he's free.

"All his life he was on a chain, near kids who were mean to him.

"No one taught him how to just be a peaceful dog.

"Well, I feel sorry for him. I'm going to sleep in the basement with him again. I just hope he doesn't breathe on me any more."

Sammy said, "Anyway, Mr. Johnson will have him tomorrow. All our troubles will be over!"

Before school the next morning, Kathy, Bill, and Sammy took Star Nose to Mr. Johnson.

Mr. Johnson took one look at the dog and said, "Where in the HECK did that thing come from? A circus?

"He looks like he's made up of parts from five different animals ... glued together.

"That's a real good-for-nothing dog you've brought me."

Star Nose was thinking, "Does this guy

mean trouble? His voice sounds loud and sort of mean. I hope he won't hurt me."

Sammy said, "He can't help how he looks. You shouldn't—"

Bill broke in, talking fast. "Good-bye, Mr. Johnson! Your yard work will be all done after school!"

Kathy and Bill grabbed Sammy. They pushed him out of the yard ... and all the way to the end of the block.

Sammy was yelling, "Stop pushing me! Especially you, Bill! I'll sock you one!"

Finally they were far enough away so Mr. Johnson couldn't hear them.

Bill said, "Sorry, Sammy. I was afraid you'd say something that would make Mr. Johnson mad."

Kathy said, "See, then he wouldn't give Star Nose a chance."

Sammy said, "I was going to tell him

Star Nose looks fine to me. I HATED
what he said.

"I've heard him talk like that before.
He doesn't like anything that looks different from what he's used to.

"He'd probably even say WE are good-
for-nothing kids!

"But if he did say that, I'd hit him
right in the nose ... POW!"

Sammy socked the air, to prove how
tough he could be.

Later that day, Mr. Johnson put Star Nose into the back seat of his four-wheel drive. Then his pointer jumped in.

Mr. Johnson headed for the farm where he hunted.

Star Nose looked at the pointer.

He thought, "I wonder if this dog knows how to have fun!"

He began jumping from the seat to the floor. Pretty soon the pointer was doing it, too.

Mr. Johnson parked his car near a field. He opened the windows. He wanted the car to be cool when he came back.

The open window gave Star Nose an idea. "Escape!" he thought.

He leaped through it and began running, fast.

The pointer jumped out after him, and disappeared from sight.

Mr. Johnson was mad.

He ran across the fields calling his pointer.   Nothing.

He searched for the dogs until noon. Nothing.

Tired and hungry, he returned to his car to eat.   He could hardly wait to get to his good meat sandwiches.

He opened the car door.

The sandwiches were gone!

Pieces of brown paper bag lay all over the front seat.

Mr. Johnson muttered, "That darn dog! He ate my lunch!"

Madder than a hornet, he started looking for the dogs again.

He found them right away.

They were near the car ... under a tree ... curled up ... sleeping off the stolen lunch.

Star Nose was snoring.

Mr. Johnson woke his dog and snapped a leash onto him.

He was so mad he thought of taking the dogs straight home. But he hated to waste the hunting trip.

He started walking with his dog.

Star Nose danced around near them.

Suddenly the pointer stood stock-still.

He smelled a pheasant.

He lifted one front paw.

He pointed his nose at a bunch of dry plants.

Star Nose thought, "What the heck is that dog doing? Doesn't he know there's a BIRD in there?" He raced right into the plants.

The pheasant flew out and hit him in the face.

Star Nose jumped in the air.

Then he fell to the ground and rolled over, flat on his back.

He had fainted.

Mr. Johnson had to pick him up and load him into the car.

He had to race back to Bluff Lake, to the animal hospital.

Chapter 10:
She Wants Him!

School was out at last.

Sammy and Bill were at Mr. Johnson's, weeding and cutting.

They were almost finished.

Sammy turned off the mower. He said, "There, I'm done with the lawn. That was a HUGE job. Ten times harder than your weeding, Bill."

Bill grinned and said, "I didn't notice you begging to trade with me ... so mine couldn't have been that easy."

He kept on weeding.

Sammy saw Bill's shirt was wet with sweat. He said, "Well, maybe your job is a LITTLE hard. And you're not nearly as strong as I am. So I'll help you, poor baby."

Just then a car drove up the driveway.

Mr. Johnson jumped out.

He lifted Star Nose out of the back seat.

He ran up to the boys.

He said, "HERE, take this poor excuse for a dog! Get him out of my sight, and do it fast!"

Bill said, "But I'm not done with the weeding."

Mr. Johnson said, "Forget the weeding! Just take him away.

"Some HUNTING dog! He fainted when he saw a pheasant. I just paid a vet good money to snap him out of it. What a useless mutt!"

He pushed Star Nose into Bill's sweaty arms. Then he stamped into his house and slammed the door.

The boys carried Star Nose home. They felt terrible.

Bill said, "Well, we've got to give him another bath. He's covered with burrs and dirt again."

They took him inside.

Mop was over-joyed to see Star Nose.

He stood with his paws on the edge of the tub, to watch the bath.

Bill lifted Star Nose out.

91

Mop barked to his friend.

Star Nose thought, "Oh, boy! Play time!"

Slippery as a fish, he wiggled loose. He ran down the hall and jumped, SPLOOSH, onto Mrs. Tandy's bed.

They had to change the bed.

Then the boys told the others how mad Mr. Johnson had been.

They all felt really bad.

Mrs. Tandy said, "Well, I think one of us should call Mr. Johnson. By now he's had a chance to cool down. We can find out what went wrong."

Dave said, "Why don't you take on that job, Mrs. T.? At least we know he likes your pies."

When Mrs. Tandy came back from the phone, she picked up Star Nose and hugged him.

She said, "Well, we may have to work

on Star Nose. We know he's not so hot as a guard dog ... he hides in closets.

"And he's not so good as a yard dog ... he runs away.

"And wait till you hear what he did as a hunting dog!"

Star Nose licked her face, SLURP, before she could duck.

Kathy had to dry Mrs. Tandy off with a paper towel.

Then Mrs. Tandy told them about the pheasant ... and the fainting ... and the meat sandwiches.

Sammy said, "Well, I don't care what Mr. Johnson says! Right now, this minute, we are going to find Star Nose a home ... and with someone a lot better than that ratty Mr. Johnson.

"Let's take those posters around this afternoon. Maybe that will work after all. Did you get them from the copy place, Mrs. Tandy?"

Mrs. Tandy said, "Here they are!"

She brought a stack of papers to the kitchen table.

Dave said, "I'll drive some of them up to the stores in Green Forest. Want to go with me, Kathy?"

Kathy smiled and nodded.

She said, "There are about a hundred sheets, and five of us. So we can each take twenty.

"And everybody, take tape with you to put them up with."

Mrs. Tandy said, "How about if I pass mine out around the neighborhood? I can go to all the houses we missed on Sunday."

She counted out twenty sheets.

Bill said, "Sammy and I can put ours in store windows in Bluff Lake. Drop us off, will you, Dave?"

Sammy said, "Count out our sheets, Bill."

Bill counted out forty sheets.

Sammy grabbed a bag of bananas.

He said, "Can't take a chance on running out of energy!"

Bill said, "And perfect food for a monkey. Let's go!"

By 6:00 they had passed out all their sheets, and were all back home.

Dave said, "Let's whip up some dinner, fast."

Sammy said, "I get to choose two cans of soup to mix. Kathy did it last time."

He stirred together cream of chicken and beef-vegetable.

They made turkey sandwiches.

Sammy tasted his soup and said, "Wow! I'm a great cook! I'm starving, and as tired as an old horse. Am I glad to be done with everything for the day!"

Dave said, "But we aren't done. We have to phone our friends about Star Nose ... and get the word around."

So after dinner, Dave, Bill, Sammy,

and Kathy took turns on the phone.

Then Mrs. Tandy made her first call.

She talked for only a minute or two, then hung up slowly.

She said, "Kids, there must be some mistake!

"I called my friend Benita Rockwell.

"I told her about Star Nose needing a home.

"I told her about all the terrible things he does.

"And you're not going to believe this!

"She WANTS him!

"WE'VE FOUND A HOME FOR STAR NOSE!"

She grabbed hold of Sammy.

The two of them danced from one end of the house to the other.

Chapter 11:
Poor Mrs. Rockwell

After school on Tuesday they drove to Mrs. Rockwell's huge old white house.

Mrs. Rockwell was sixty-five years old. She was tiny. "Ninety pounds soaking wet," Mrs. Tandy said.

She had known Benita for years. They met at a bake sale, and liked each other right away.

Mrs. Rockwell loved the Woodlanders, too. Today she was waiting for them at the front door.

She saw they had left Star Nose in the station wagon.

She said, "Where's my new dog? Still in the car? Bring him here, for goodness sakes!

"You can't imagine how often I've thought of having a dog again. But I just didn't do it.

"Your phone call solved the problem! Now I'll have a darling animal to keep me company!"

The Woodlanders looked at each other when she said the word DARLING.

Mrs. Tandy said, "But, Benita, what

about all the things I told you, the trouble he gets into?"

Mrs. Rockwell said, "Oh, Becky. He doesn't sound so bad to me ... just full of spirit ... sort of a Sammy of the dog world."

She patted Sammy on the head, even though he was as tall as she was. She said, "Now will some one PLEASE bring me my dog?"

Bill ran to the car.

He led Star Nose back on a chain leash.

Mrs. Rockwell sat down on the front step to get closer to the dog.

Star Nose looked at her and growled a little.

He thought, "Who's this new person? Should I trust her or not? Does she have food or doesn't she?"

Bill said, "I bet he thinks you're a kid,

you're so little. He's scared of kids. He used to live with some who were mean to him."

Mrs. Rockwell held out a hand for Star Nose to sniff.

Then she scratched his nose.

Then he let her scratch his ears.

The next thing they knew, he put his front paws on her lap. Then he smiled right in her face!

Star Nose was thinking, "I like her! She looks like a push-over!"

Mrs. Rockwell said, "My, my! He can smile, just like a person! I've never heard of a dog who could do that. He IS a darling animal!"

Even the Woodlanders were starting to think so.

Then Star Nose moved right into her lap, and let her rub his back.

Sammy said, "He LIKES you!"

He ran to the car and brought out some bags.

He said, "Mrs. Tandy shopped for these while we were in school. We asked her to buy that chain leash ... so he wouldn't be able to chew through it."

Dave said, "And here's a food bowl and a water bowl. They're the kind that a dog can't tip over. But if I know Star Nose, he will find a way."

Kathy said, "And here's a flea collar ... and some cans of dog food .. and a bag of dry food, too."

Bill said, "And here's dog shampoo. If he keeps on acting up, you'll need a lot of this."

Mrs. Tandy said, "And here's a dog tag. We put his name on it, with your phone number."

Sammy said, "And here's his blanket. He likes to sleep with it. But we didn't buy him a bed. He likes to choose where he sleeps."

Mrs. Rockwell laughed. She said, "This porch looks like a pet store.

"Well, I have a present for him, too. It's in the backyard. In fact, it's PART of the backyard.

"I had a little dog yard built years ago, when I had my last dog. Now Star Nose can have it."

She took them around to her big backyard. She led Star Nose into a little fenced-in part, just outside the back door.

She said, "We can leave him out here for now. He can get used to his new running space. Let's go in and talk ... and drink some lemonade!"

They took Dave up the steps in his chair.

Inside Mrs. Rockwell said, "My grandchildren are coming Saturday afternoon for an over-night visit.

"Do you think you could all come Saturday night for a sleeping-bag party?

"We can do it the way we did last time. Kathy and Annie and Julie can put sleeping bags in the playroom.

"You boys and Timmy can camp in the biggest guest room.

"Becky and I can use my room."

Sammy said, "Hey, that sounds great!"

They all loved the idea.

Bill asked, "What time should we come over?"

Mrs. Rockwell said, "How about five o'clock? I'll buy hamburgers and hot dogs and corn. We can barbecue dinner on the grill."

They finished making their plans. Then they went out the back door to say good-bye to Star Nose.

But they just stood and stared.

"Holy cow!"

"Lucky we came out!"

"That rat!"

"Grab him before he gets away!"

The fence around the dog yard was made of wooden sticks.

Star Nose had been busy chewing. He had chewed the bottoms off two of them.

He had wiggled halfway through the hole he had made.

Sammy and Bill ran and pulled him back in.

Then Sammy turned to Mrs. Rockwell.

He looked worried.

He said, "He broke your dog yard! Now I bet you won't want to keep him! Just when we thought we found a good home for him, too."

But Mrs. Rockwell said, "Nonsense, Sammy! Of COURSE I want to keep him.

"My gardener comes tomorrow. I'll just ask him to line the bottom of the fence with chicken wire.

"Then Star Nose couldn't possibly get into any other trouble."

Kathy moaned to herself, "Poor, trusting Mrs. Rockwell."

Chapter 12:
The Biter

The next day, Wednesday, the gardener came to work.

He put chicken wire inside the fence.

He wired it to the bottom.

Mrs. Rockwell played with Star Nose and fed him.

She took him walking down the block on his new leash.

She let him sniff at every tree and bush and flower.

She let him sniff at every passing dog.

Then she took him home and ate her lunch.

Then she brushed Star Nose.

She gave him a doggy treat.

She patted his tummy.

She gave him a toy, a hard rubber ball.

For hours she threw the ball across the living room for him to chase.

Star Nose thought, "I hope she never stops! Keep throwing it, keep throwing it!"

Finally it was dinner time. Mrs. Rockwell said, "There, you must be all worn-out! I bet you will be a good dog now!"

Star Nose couldn't figure out why she had stopped throwing the ball.

She fed him.   She put him into the dog yard and ate her own dinner.

She answered some letters.

At 8:30 she went to bring Star Nose in.

She found out he had dug a hole a foot deep, down under the chicken wire. He was almost out of the yard again!

She pulled him out of the hole.   She took him into the house.

She gave him his blanket and doggy treat.

Then, all worn-out herself, she went to sleep.

Thursday morning she asked her gardener to dig a deep trench.

He dug a trench one foot deep ... all along the inside of the dog-yard fence.

He stood a metal liner in the trench. From the bottom of the fence it ran straight into the ground ... one foot down.

By Thursday evening Star Nose had dug four deep holes. He couldn't get through the metal liner!

Star Nose thought, "Rats! I guess I have to find some other way to escape!"

So he stopped digging and took a running leap over the fence.

He landed in the big backyard. He was FREE!

Mrs. Rockwell happened to see him from the window.

She darted out the back door.

She held a big, juicy beef bone out to him.

Star Nose decided to stick around. He took the bone and let her lead him into the house.

Mrs. Rockwell's gardener came again on Friday.

He hammered long sticks into the ground all around the dog yard.

He nailed chicken wire to them to make the fence taller.

Now Star Nose couldn't jump over.

So he tried again to dig under. No luck.

He jumped again.

Then he dug again until he was tired ... and grumpy ... and hungry.

He decided he didn't like Mrs. Rockwell anymore.

He ran around the dog yard. He wouldn't let her catch him to go inside.

Finally she stopped trying.

From her pocket she took a doggy

treat. She held it up.

He sniffed at it. He thought, "I want it, but she just wants to catch me again."

Finally he growled ... and darted up ... and grabbed the doggy treat ... and ran back away from her ... and munched it.

She hadn't tried to catch him. He was still hungry ... and now she was holding up another treat.

He walked over slowly. He grabbed it. He munched it down.

She patted him.

Star Nose wondered, "Does she have another treat?" He put his head against her knee.

She snapped the leash onto his collar.

He thought, "Trapped! She caught me! Well, too bad for her!"

She tried to lead him to the back door. He planted all four paws on the ground.   He held his legs stiff.

He wouldn't move them.

Mrs. Rockwell dragged him with her. It was like dragging a little table.

His toe nails dug through the grass.

Finally she dragged him, growling, through the door.   She closed it.

She took his leash off.

The dog thought, "I'm free! I'm free!" He rushed from the kitchen into the dining room.

He leaped up onto the antique dinner table.

He jumped down and ran into the living room, onto the couch.

He knocked a vase off the coffee table as he leaped to a chair.

He darted onto the inside porch and banged into a floor lamp.

He raced upstairs into every bedroom, onto every bed.

He heard Mrs. Rockwell call his name.

He thought, "Hmm ... I'll run downstairs for a second and see if she has any more treats for me." He raced to the kitchen.

There stood Mrs. Rockwell with his bowl full of dog food. But behind her, on the counter, something smelled BETTER.

So he jumped onto the counter.

He grabbed one end of the good-smelling thing and ran.

It was a string of chubby hot dogs, fastened together end-to-end.

He chewed on one as the others bounced along after him.

He pulled them up the stairs.

He stopped for a minute to get another one into his mouth.

He thought, "Someone might try to take this away from me. I'll hide."

He dragged them under a bed. He held them with his paws.

Mrs. Rockwell knew Star Nose would be sick if he ate the whole chain of hot dogs. So she followed him into the bedroom.

She saw a hot dog sticking out from under the bed.

She reached down and pulled on it.

Star Nose felt the hot dog under his paws move.

He zoomed out from under the bed.

He bit down hard on the thing that was pulling his hot dogs.

Blood dripped from Mrs. Rockwell's hand onto the rug!

Chapter 13:
The Good-for-Something Dog

The next evening the Woodlanders drove up to Mrs. Rockwell's house.

They had Mop on a leash.

Mrs. Rockwell met them at the door.

Her grandchildren were waiting just inside.

Right away three-year-old Annie said, "Bad dog eat Gram-a."

They saw Mrs. Rockwell's hand, wrapped up in a bandage.

Mrs. Tandy said, "Benita! My lands! What have we gotten you into! I'll never forgive myself. We will take Star Nose right home. We—"

Mrs. Rockwell said, "Now, calm down, Becky."

Then she turned and whistled and called, "Here, Star Nose!"

Star Nose trotted out from under the dining-room table.

He licked the hand that Mrs. Rockwell reached down to him.

He went over to lick Mop on the nose, but they didn't start racing around.

Mrs. Rockwell said, "I scolded him

after he bit me.

"He was so ashamed he hid in the closet. It was two hours before I could get him to come out.

"He's just never had anyone to teach him before. He has to learn how to be a good dog, and he will.

"And Becky, don't fret about the safety of the children. I told them to leave him alone unless he comes up to be petted.

"He's already gone to each one. He's been as sweet as honey. He really deserves a chance.

"So let's go and barbecue!"

Now it was 9:00. Kathy and ten-year-old Julie got into their pajamas. Then they called Annie.

She answered from her grandmother's room. "Coming. Done wif my job on Star Nose." (She had a little trouble saying words with TH in them.)

Julie said, "Uh-oh. What job is she talking about?"

Annie came in smiling.

She said, "Look at dis dog. Come here, honey baby puppy."

Star Nose trotted in.

Kathy said, "Oh my gosh. Look at his toenails!"

Annie had painted them with bright pink nail polish.

She said proudly, "And I didn't spill on ANYfing!"

Star Nose stood still and smiled.

At bedtime Bill took Mop into the boys' room and closed the door.

He told six-year-old Timmy, "This way the dogs won't get into trouble together tonight."

Star Nose dragged his blanket into Mrs. Rockwell's bedroom. He pulled it up onto her bed and went to sleep.

At 3:00 in the morning he rushed out into the hall, barking.

He began scratching madly on the boys' bedroom door.

He ran back and jumped onto Mrs. Rockwell's bed.

Then he jumped to the other bed ... right onto Mrs. Tandy's stomach!

He ran into the hall again and hurled himself at the boys' door.

Timmy whined, half-asleep, "That bad dog! Make him stop!"

Sammy said sleepily, "Maybe there's something wrong ... SOMETHING WRONG! Bill! Dave! WAKE UP!"

Bill leaped out of bed.

Dave was already in his chair. He shouted, "Quick, Sammy, open our door!"

The boys rushed out into the hall.

The smell of smoke came from under the girls' bedroom door.

Bill threw the door open.

Kathy, Julie, and Annie sat up in their sleeping bags.

A small lamp on the table near the window had been left on. Smoke was curling out from its shade.

Kathy reached over right away and pulled the lamp plug out of the wall.

Dave shouted, "Quick! Get it away from those curtains! And get it wet before the shade bursts into flames!"

Sammy grabbed the lamp.

He ran into the bathroom and stuffed
it shade-first into the TOILET!

Annie went over to him. She said,
"Boy, is Gram-a going to be MAD at you!
Wait till she comes into dis BAFroom!"

At that moment, Mrs. Rockwell and
Mrs. Tandy came running in.

Mrs. Rockwell said, "What's happened?
Something's burning!"

Bill patted her arm. He said, "Don't worry. It's OK now. Star Nose woke us up in time. The lamp was on fire, but we took care of it."

Annie said, "I fink you should get mad at Sammy. He frew your lamp right in the TOILET."

Timmy came stumbling in. He was still half-asleep. He grumbled, "That good-for-nothing dog woke me up."

Mrs. Rockwell laughed and said, "You won't understand until you're awake, Timmy. But Star Nose is far from a good-for-nothing dog.

"In fact, he's the best dog anyone could ever have!

"He's a STAR! In fact, from now on, that's his new name. Star. Just plain Star. We can even get a new name tag made for him.

"He has a home with me as long as

he lives.

"Good doggy. Good Star."

Everybody petted him and called him a good dog.

Star thought, "Yipee! They like me! Maybe they'll feed me a treat!"

He loved all the excitement. He ran up to Mop. He bit his neck.

He started a mad race through the house, just like he used to.

So everybody stayed up.

They went downstairs.

Mrs. Rockwell took out the cookie jar ... and some doggy treats ... and poured some milk.

Then they sat down for a party in the middle of the night.

Sammy sneaked a doggy treat onto Bill's plate, to trick him into eating it.

But Sammy was so tired, he ate it himself by mistake!

And Star, the good-for-something dog, stood watching ... and smiling!

He thought, "I guess these people are OK after all."